Cat and Mouse

Learn the Colors!

Written by **Stéphane Husar**
Illustrated by **Loïc Méhée**

www.av2books.com

Go to **www.av2books.com**, and enter this book's unique code.

BOOK CODE

Z258982

AV² by Weigl brings you media enhanced books that support active learning.

First Published by

Your AV² Media Enhanced book gives you a fiction readalong online. Log on to **www.av2books.com** and enter the unique book code from page 2 to use your readalong.

AV² Readalong Navigation

HIGHLIGHTED TEXT

HOME

CLOSE

START READING
READ

PAGE TURNING
BACK NEXT

TITLE INFORMATION
INFO

PAGE PREVIEW

Published by AV² by Weigl
350 5ᵗʰ Avenue, 59ᵗʰ Floor New York, NY 10118
Websites: www.av2books.com   www.weigl.com

Printed in the United States of America in Brainerd, Minnesota
1 2 3 4 5 6 7 8 9 0 19 18 17 16 15

042015
WEP021715

Library of Congress Control Number: 2015934107

ISBN 978-1-4896-3813-7 (hardcover)
ISBN 978-1-4896-3814-4 (single user eBook)
ISBN 978-1-4896-3815-1 (multi-user eBook)

Text copyright ©2010 by ABC MELODY.
Illustrations copyright ©2010 by ABC MELODY.
Published in 2010 by ABC MELODY.

ABC MELODY Éditions
26, rue Liancourt 75014
Paris, France

Cat and Mouse

Learn the Colors!

Written by **Stéphane Husar**

Illustrated by **Loïc Méhée**

www.av2books.com

It's a **blue** balloon.

6

It's a **green** balloon.

8

It's a **red** balloon.

Hi Cat!
Look at
the balloon!

What color
is it?

11

Hi Cat!
Look at
the balloon!

What color
is it?

12

It's a **white** balloon.

Hi Cat! Look at the balloon!

What color is it?

14

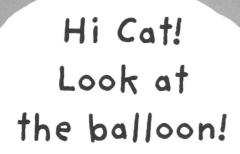

20

21

Hi Cat!
Look at
the balloon!

What color
is it?

It's an **orange** balloon.

Hey, Mouse,
there's no balloon
on this page...

Cat and Mouse's French-English Phrasebook

Learn the colors!: Apprends les couleurs!

Hi!: Salut!

Look at the balloon!: Regarde le ballon!

What color is it?: De quelle couleur est-il?/
Quelle couleur est-ce?

It's a blue balloon.: C'est un ballon bleu.

There's no balloon on this page!:
Il n'y a pas de ballon sur cette page!

Would you like a balloon?:
Voulez-vous un ballon?/Veux-tu un ballon?

blue: bleu

red: rouge

green: vert

yellow: jaune

white: blanc

pink: rose

brown: marron

black: noir

purple: violet

orange: orange

gray: gris

28